Cecelia the Seal

Gets a Meal!

by Jim Coogan

Harvest Home Books

For Annah and Elsa – two close friends

Published by Harvest Home Books
Post Office Box 1181
East Dennis, Massachusetts 02641

ISBN 978-0-9893073-1-4

Cover and page layout by KVH Graphic Design, Mashpee, Massachusetts

Printed in the United States of America

Additional titles published by Harvest Home Books may be viewed and ordered through our website
www.harvesthomebooks.com

Bulk discounts are available for institutions and non-profit organizations.

Seals are found all along the shores of
Cape Cod and the Islands.

Gray seals like to haul out on the beach and bask in the sun.

Harbor seals prefer to rest on rocks just off shore. From a distance they look like bananas.

3

Cecelia is a little harbor seal. Sometimes she joins her gray seal cousins on the beach. But mostly she stays in the water.

On land, seals are clumsy and awkward. But in the water, they are like ballerinas – graceful and nimble swimmers.

Seals like to swim after fish because fish are their favorite food.

6

When there are lots of fish
around, seal tummies are full.

7

But others like fish too and often there are not enough to go around.

8

Sometimes when Cecelia caught a fish, she didn't always get to keep it.

9

Many nights Cecelia went to sleep
with an empty tummy.

One morning something unusual woke Cecelia up. It was the strong smell of fish – lots and lots of fish!!!

Cecelia started to follow that fishy smell. She swam in the direction where it was coming from.

12

She came to a wide stream. The smell of
fish was much stronger now.

But which way to go? The stream went in many directions.

Cecelia kept following her nose until she came to a town.

But there were no fish there.

16

Cecelia tried other streams. Finally she found one that went under a road and a railroad track. On the other side was a very strange little village.

17

No one seemed to be home. Cecelia thought that maybe whoever lived there came out of the little holes at night to sit and have tea on their nice green lawns.

Beyond the village the stream went into a pipe.
Cecelia was sure the fish must be on the other side.

CLOSED
FOR THE
SEASON

← FIRST HOLE

It was now late in the afternoon. The smell of fish was really strong. There was nothing left for Cecelia to do but to go through that pipe. And so she did.

KEEP OUT
FISH
HATCHERY

On the other side, the stream continued into some woods.

Cecelia soon came to a long and narrow pond. It was full of fish!!! This is what she had been smelling.

It was easy to move the net that covered the pond. Cecelia swam inside. There were so many fish that Cecelia couldn't count them. She ate lots of fish. That night Cecelia did not go to sleep with an empty tummy. In fact, she never went to sleep at all!!!

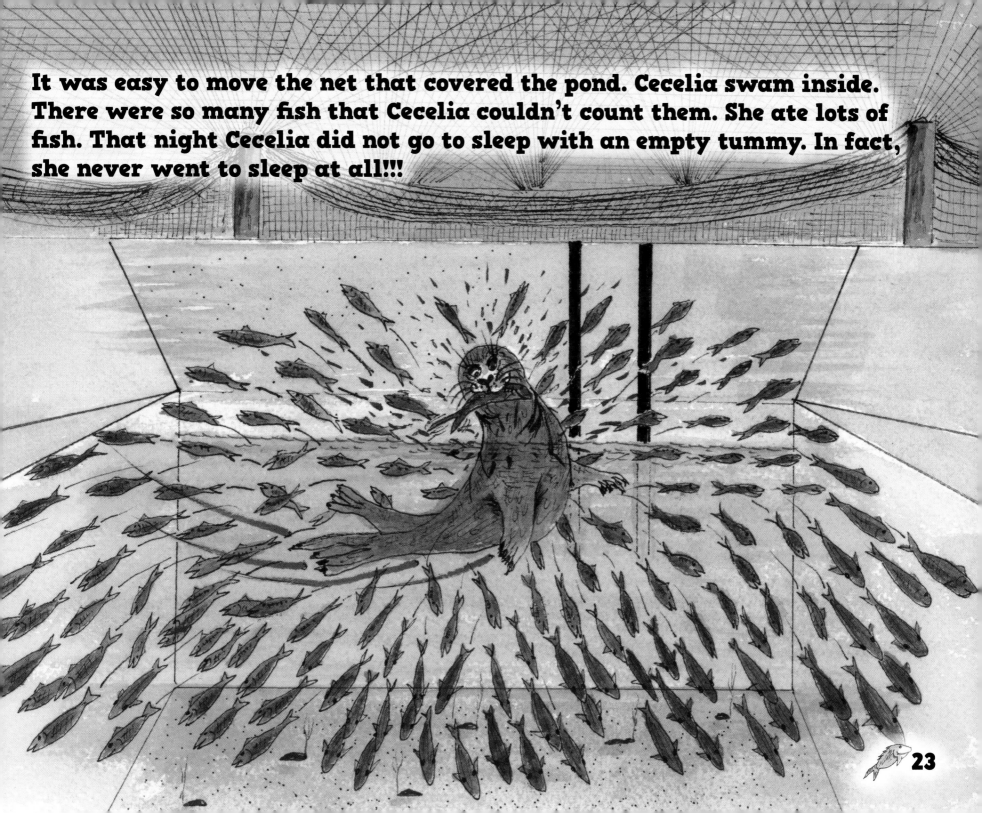

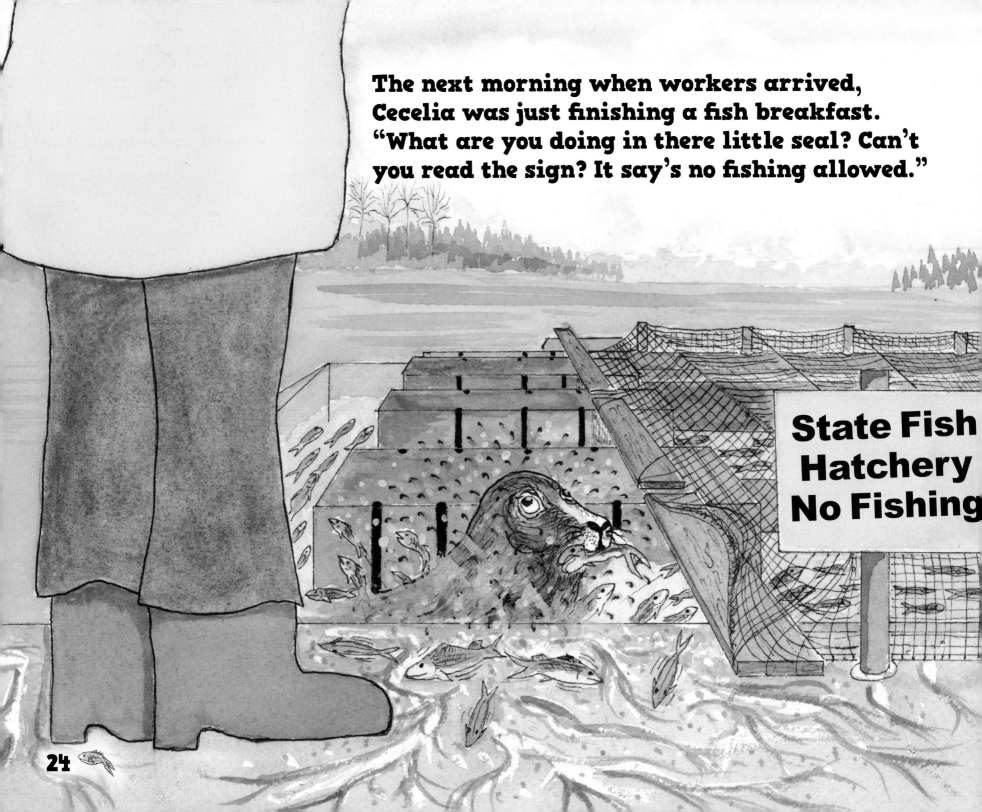

The next morning when workers arrived, Cecelia was just finishing a fish breakfast. "What are you doing in there little seal? Can't you read the sign? It say's no fishing allowed."

State Fish Hatchery No Fishing

24

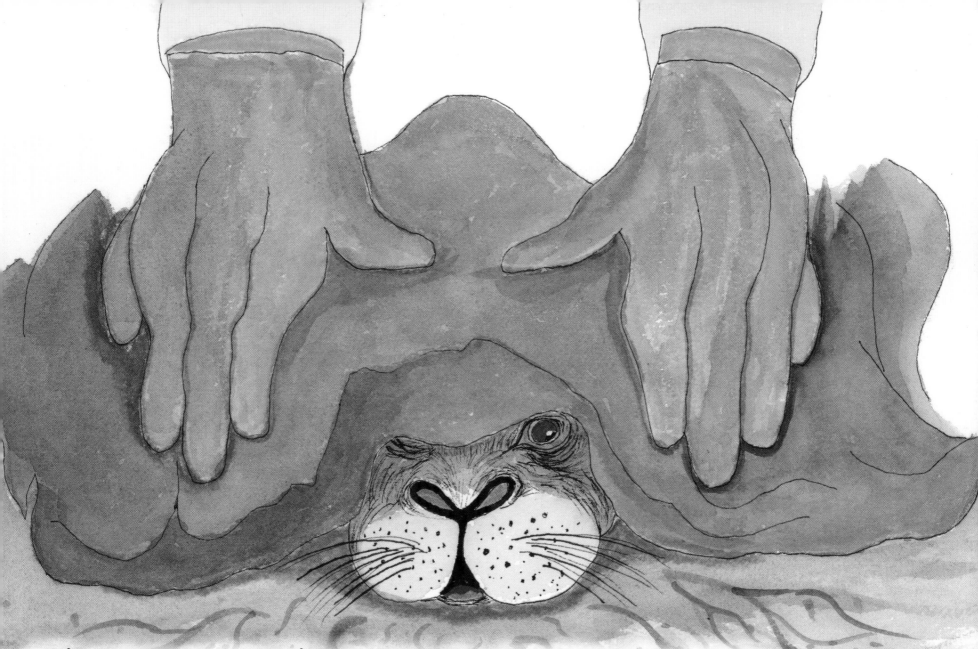

A big net scooped Cecelia up. Strong hands held her down and a blanket was put over her head. The little seal was very tired. And she had a very bad tummy ache from eating all those fish. Cecelia was put into a truck and taken away from the fish pond.

At a beach far away, Cecelia was pushed out of the truck. "Don't come back, little seal! Go find somewhere else to fish!!!

The new beach was better than the old one. The water was deep and clear and there were lots of other seals to play with. And best of all, Cecelia's new home had what seals really like - lots and lots of fish. What could be better than that?

Facts about Harbor Seals

Harbor seals are the second most common type of seal found in New England waters behind the gray seal. They are a year-round presence along shore and are seen in all seasons. Preferring outlying rocks, rather than hauling up on the beach like their gray seal cousins, harbor seals can be spotted sleeping and sunning on these outcroppings. The color of harbor seals is not uniform and can vary with the seasons from light gray, to brown and even black. They are generally spotted all over their bodies and at maturity can weigh 150-200 pounds with a body length of 4-5 feet. Early mariners tagged these seals with the nickname "sea dog" because their faces very much resemble common domestic dogs.

Can you help Cecelia get a meal?

In January of 2009, workers arriving early at the Sandwich Fish Hatchery were surprised to find a little harbor seal happily munching on the trout that are raised at the facility. She had worked her way almost two miles inland from Cape Cod Bay through a maze of tidal channels and a pipe under Route 6A to reach what to her was an all-you-can-eat self-serve, fresh fish restaurant. The seal was less than a year old and weighed about forty pounds – several of which probably were gained during her hours of feasting on some of the larger brood fish in the fish farm.

Members of the Cape Cod Stranding Network were called to the hatchery where the little seal was netted and put into an animal carrier. The seal was put into a truck and taken to a beach on the south side of Cape Cod – far away from the hatchery. There, after being tagged for identification, the animal was released back into the water with the hope she would not return to Sandwich. Apparently none the worse for her night in trout heaven, the little seal paddled off in search of, what else? More fish!!!

To view Cecelia's adventure, go online to: The seal who came to dinner in Sandwich, Massachusetts.